KBUG Radio

UP CLOSE AND PERSONAL

KBUG Radio

UP CLOSE AND PERSONAL

An Interview with

Harry
the Tarantula

Leigh Ann Tyson

illustrated by **Henrik Drescher**

NATIONAL GEOGRAPHIC

WASHINGTON, D.C.

Good day to you. You are listening to UP CLOSE AND PERSONAL and I am Katy Did on KBUG radio, bringing you the latest chirp. And what a fine day it is, for we are fortunate to have here with us in our studio Harry Spyder, who is a tarantula from California. Harry has been so kind to take time out of his busy schedule and spend a few moments chatting with us.

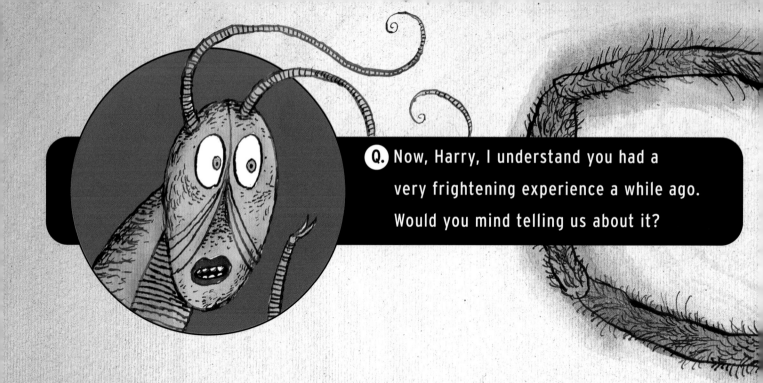

Q. Now, Harry, I understand you had a very frightening experience a while ago. Would you mind telling us about it?

A. Oh sure. I didn't mean to scare her, but she took me by surprise. I lost quite a lot of hair on my back because of it. Pretty soon I'll be bald. Look at me. I'm still shaking.

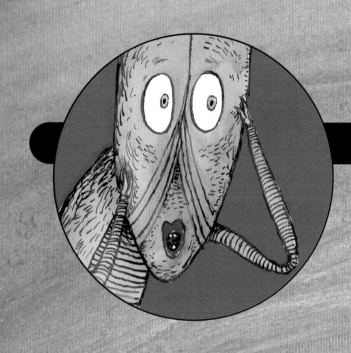

Q. What do you mean?

A. A little girl named Laura Webber scooped me into an empty bottle. When she opened the lid, I looked up out of the bottle with my eight eyes and saw a huge face staring right at me. I nearly jumped out of my skin.

A. I did what any tarantula would do. I leaned back on my hind legs, lifted my front ones up, and opened my fangs in horror. Then I reached around with my front legs and rubbed some hairs off my back and tried to fling them at her.

A. Well, I'll tell you. It usually makes scary animals go away. I think my hair irritates them. Have you ever looked closely at tarantula hairs? They're really very nice. I'm quite proud of them.

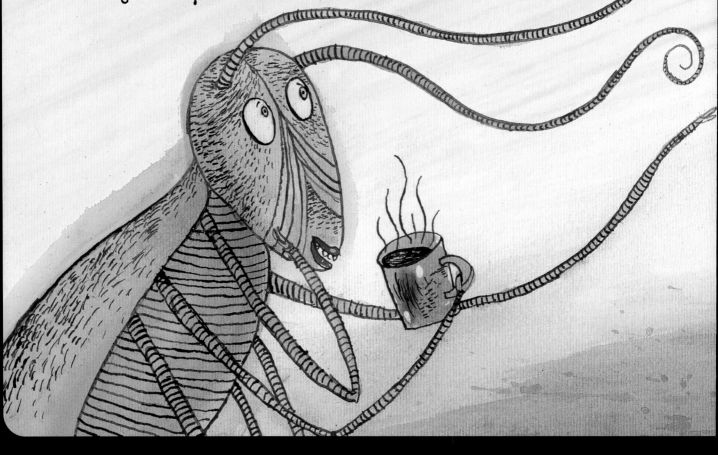

Q. Could I look at one now?

A. You mean, like, take one out? No, I couldn't. I never know when I might need them. And I have shed my skin for the last time. So I won't have any more hair. I hardly have any left now.

Q. Do you know why your hair might irritate someone?

A. I think it's the barbs. Each one of my hairs has teeny tiny barbs. Animals breathe them in, then they snort and snort. Ha! Good luck making a meal out of me.

Close-up of Harry's hair

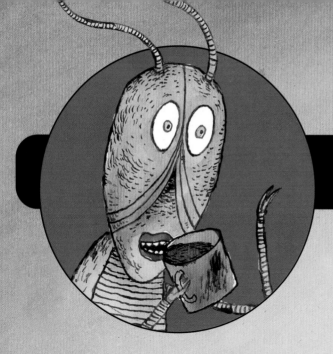

A. Because I was growing. I'm now three inches across, the biggest I'll ever be. I understand my cousins down south grow even bigger. They can be about ten inches across. They also catch and eat mice. Ah, what a life.

go Harry go!

A. Mostly crickets. But I also like to eat beetles, grasshoppers, and millipedes. Burp. Excuse me. I just ate a cricket a little while ago.

A. Yes, it's true. Isn't it marvelous? In one bite I can paralyze a cricket, and the poison will turn it into a very juicy morsel. I'm getting hungry just thinking about it.

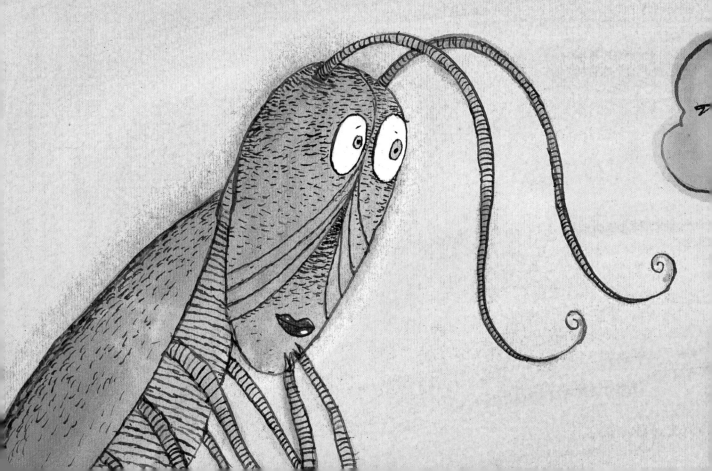

Q. It says here in my notes that you bit the girl that caught you. That girl called Laura Webber?

A. No, I didn't bite her. That's just a rumor. But even if I did, my poison wouldn't do much to her. It would probably just make a sore lump on her skin.

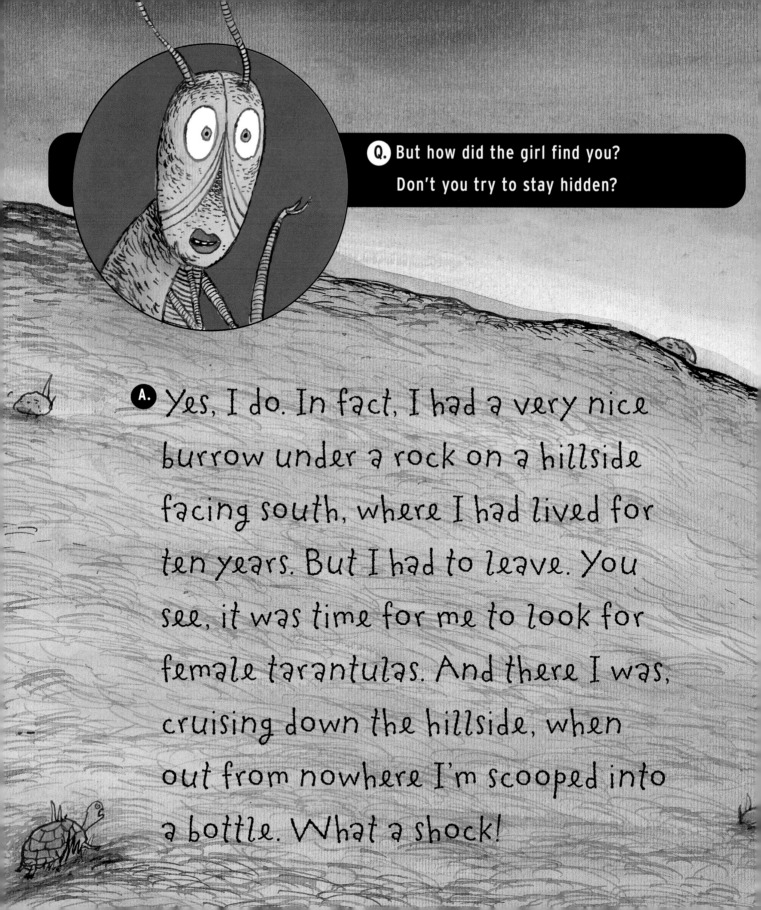

Q. But how did the girl find you? Don't you try to stay hidden?

A. Yes, I do. In fact, I had a very nice burrow under a rock on a hillside facing south, where I had lived for ten years. But I had to leave. You see, it was time for me to look for female tarantulas. And there I was, cruising down the hillside, when out from nowhere I'm scooped into a bottle. What a shock!

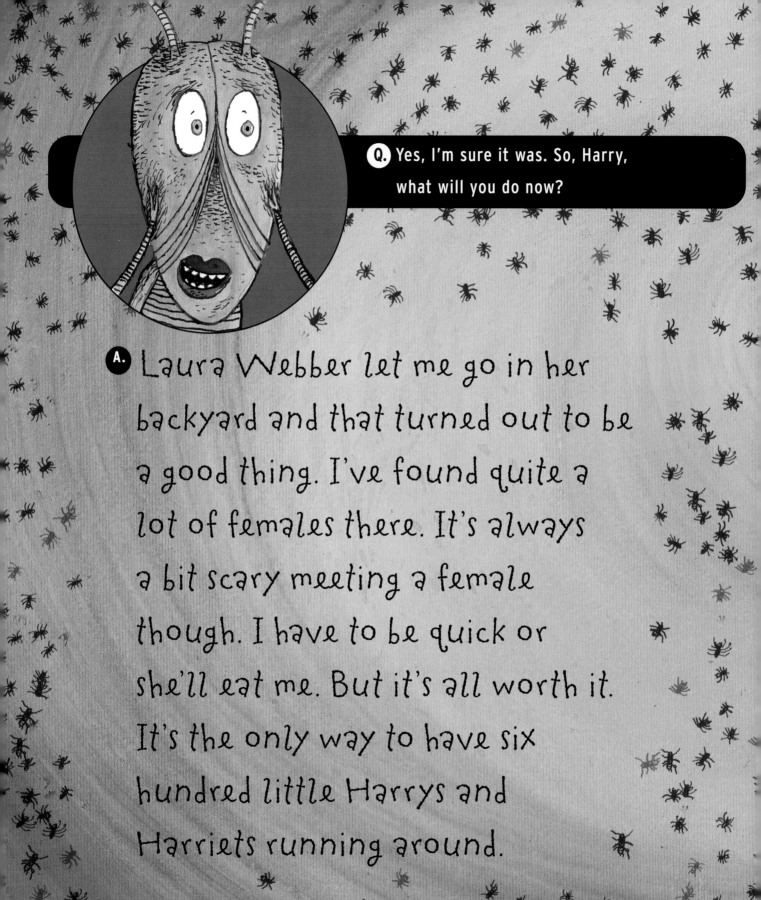

Q. Yes, I'm sure it was. So, Harry, what will you do now?

A. Laura Webber let me go in her backyard and that turned out to be a good thing. I've found quite a lot of females there. It's always a bit scary meeting a female though. I have to be quick or she'll eat me. But it's all worth it. It's the only way to have six hundred little Harrys and Harriets running around.

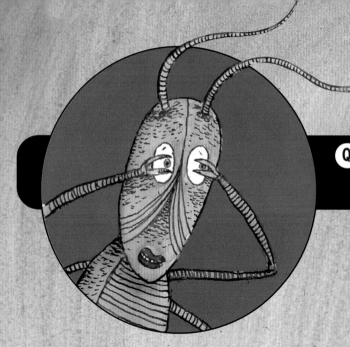

Q. What do you do that you have to be quick about, if you don't mind my asking?

A. I have to transfer my web sack of sperm to her. I must be very careful and tap her in all the right places. Tapping puts her in a romantic mood. Then I transfer my sack, and I'm out of there in a flash. So far, so good. I can thank my lucky stars.

And that was Harry the Tarantula, and this is Katy Did with UP CLOSE AND PERSONAL on KBUG radio. Until next time, good-bye.

Tarantula Facts

*T*arantulas mostly eat insects. Species that [live] in rain forests also feed on frogs, toads, mi[ce] and other small animals. Some tarantulas [can] survive on water alone for about three ye[ars]

*T*he biggest spiders in the world are tarantulas.

*T*arantulas have small hairs on their feet that help them climb with ease.

A tarantula's bite can be painful, but its venom is not deadly to humans.

*T*here are about 850 kinds of tarantulas. They live on every continent except Antarctica.

*T*arantulas live in a variety of habitats, from steamy rain forests to dry deserts.

*I*n tropical regions, some kinds of tarantulas live in trees.

*M*ost tarantulas live in holes they dig, called burrows. Sometimes they dig their burrows beneath rocks. Burrows are often located on hillsides.

*M*ost [have] entranc[es] with webs [...]

Tarantulas can run very fast, although not for very long at a time. They do not jump.

In the American Southwest, male tarantulas are sometimes seen crossing highways in huge numbers as they wander in search of females.

A female tarantula spins a patch of silk in her burrow on which to lay her eggs. Once she has finished laying the eggs, she forms the silk into a sack-like container.

Female tarantulas may lay 80 to more than 1000 eggs. The mother tarantula guards the egg sack until the baby tarantulas hatch and leave the burrow.

Near a tarantula's head are the pedipalps, which look like two little legs. They help the spider eat.

s line the burrows spin.

In cold climates, tarantulas stay in their burrows throughout the winter. They sometimes plug the opening to the burrow with webs, leaves, and soil.

The tarantula's enemies include skunks, birds, lizards, frogs, toads, snakes, wasps, and other tarantulas.

To my parents, Jerry and Claudia.
—LAT

To Sofia and Emile.
—HD

Text copyright © 2003 Leigh Ann Tyson Schmuttenmaer
Illustrations copyright © 2003 Henrik Drescher

Book design by Bea Jackson
Katy Did's voice is set in Interstate Regular Condensed,
designed by Tobias Frere-Jones with Cyrus Highsmith for Font Bureau.
Harry's voice is set in ITC Tapioca, designed by Eric Stevens.

Acknowledgments: The author gives special thanks to her husband and
children, and to her writing group for their generous support.

Library of Congress Cataloging-in-Publication Data
Tyson, Leigh Ann.
An interview with Harry the Tarantula / by Leigh Ann Tyson ;
illustrated by Henrik Drescher.
p. cm.
Summary: Katy Did of KBUG Radio interviews Harry about a recent adventure
and, in the process, finds out a lot about tarantulas.
ISBN 0-7922-5122-9 (hard cover)
[1. Tarantulas--Fiction. 2. Radio--Fiction. 3. Insects--Fiction.] I. Drescher,
Henrik, ill. II. Title.
PZ7.T985 2003
[E]--dc21
2002154399

One of the world's largest nonprofit scientific and educational organizations, the National
Geographic Society was founded in 1888 "for the increase and diffusion of geographic
knowledge." Fulfilling this mission, the Society educates and inspires millions every day
through its magazines, books, television programs, videos, maps and atlases, research
grants, the National Geographic Bee, teacher workshops, and innovative classroom
materials. The Society is supported through membership dues, charitable gifts, and income
from the sale of its educational products. This support is vital to National Geographic's
mission to increase global understanding and promote conservation of our planet through
exploration, research, and education.

For more information, please call 1-800-NGS LINE (647-5463) or write to the
following address:

NATIONAL GEOGRAPHIC SOCIETY
1145 17th Street N.W.
Washington, D.C. 20036-4688 U.S.A.

Visit the Society's Web site: www.nationalgeographic.com

About the Consultants

David W. Inouye is an ecologist and conservation biologist at the University of Maryland. He has studied insects and wildflowers at the Rocky Mountain Biological Laboratory since 1971. He researches ant-plant interactions and the bumblebees, hummingbirds, and flies that pollinate wildflowers that grow in the Colorado Mountains.

Brian D. Inouye is an ecologist at Florida State University. He has studied and photographed insects and spiders in North America and Central America. He currently researches parasitoids, which are insects that attack prey insects and lay eggs inside the victims. He also studies insects that cause plant galls.

Bibliography

Baerg, William J. **The Tarantula**. Lawrence, Kansas: University of Kansas Press, 1958.

Conniff, Richard. "Tarantulas." **National Geographic** (September 1996) 98-115.

Gertsch, Willis J. **American Spiders**. New York: Litton Educational Publishing, Inc., 1979.

Emerton, James H. **The Common Spiders of the United States**. New York: Dover Publications, Inc., 1961.

Marshall, Samuel D. "The Importance of Being Hairy." **Natural History** magazine (September 1992) 40-46.

Patent, Dorothy H. **The Lives of Spiders**. New York: Holiday House, 1980.

Perrero, Laurie, and Louis Perrero. **Tarantulas in Nature and as Pets**. Miami: Windward Publishing, Inc., 1979.